mindful monsters

ROAR YOUR WORRIES AWAY

Published in the UK by Scholastic Children's Books, 2021
Euston House, 24 Eversholt Street, London, NW1 1DB
A division of Scholastic Ltd

London ~ New York ~ Toronto ~ Sydney ~ Auckland
Mexico City ~ New Delhi ~ Hong Kong

SCHOLASTIC and associated logos are trademarks and/or
registered trademarks of Scholastic Inc.

Written by Rebecca Gerlings
Designed by Martin Aggett

© Mindful Monsters 2017, Scope (IP) Ltd, 2021

ISBN 978 0702 30403 3

A CIP catalogue record for this book is available from the British Library.

Printed and bound in China.
Papers used by Scholastic Children's Books are made from wood grown in sustainable forests.

2 4 6 8 10 9 7 5 3 1

www.scholastic.co.uk

It's a lovely, sunny day and little monsters **Thinky**, **Sparky**, **Giggles** and **Snug** are bursting with ideas for games to play.

Thinky wants to see how long he can balance on one leg. "Hey, look at me!" he says.

"**Wait**, I've got an idea too," says **Sparky**, waving her tentacles. "What about a dance-off?"

"**No!** A funny-face competition!" says **Giggles**, crossing his eyes and waggling his tongue.

The monsters are roaring with excitement, getting **LOUDER** and **LOUDER**.

The louder her friends get, the quieter **Snug** feels. She tries to let out a roar too, but the others can't hear her.

"We can play all the games and take it in turns!" calls **Thinky**, whizzing ahead.

Sparky and **Giggles** nod excitedly.
"That's a great idea!" they shout together.

Snug is feeling left out... She wants to play with her friends, but she's not sure if they will like her game.

First, **Thinky**, **Sparky** and **Giggles** try standing on one leg.

"Copy me," says **Thinky**. He puts out his arms and lifts one leg. "Ta-da!"

Sparky has a go too. "Whoa!" she laughs, wobbling around. One tentacle is tricky!

Giggles can't decide which of his legs to stand on! **"Ha, ha!"** he laughs, toppling over.

Snug wants to join in, but she has a wobbly, worried feeling in her tummy...

Snug shuts her eyes and takes a deep breath, catching her worry in a bubble – **bloop!** And blowing it away – **whoooooosh!**

Feeling calmer, **Snug** decides she'll use her wings to balance. She's ready to try – but it's too late.

"I'm done keeping still!" says **Sparky**. "Let's **DANCE!** Imagine we're... **jumping beans**!"

Thinky, **Sparky** and **Giggles** wiggle and boogie around. They move faster and faster until **Snug**'s head feels all spinny...

Snug shuts her eyes again and takes a deep breath, catching her worry in a bubble – **bloop!** And blowing it away – **whoooooosh!**

THUMP!

A loud noise interrupts **Snug**'s quiet time. Her friends have all fallen down.

"All that dancing has got my tentacles in a twist!" **Sparky** snorts, waving them about.

Giggles distracts **Sparky** with silly faces while **Thinky** untangles her legs. It's sooo tickly!

Snug has a tickly feeling too. But hers is in her tummy...

Everything's getting a bit too noisy and monstery for **Snug**, so she lies down on the grass.

"Catch the worry – **bloop!**
And blow it away – **whoooooosh!**"
she breathes.

"What game are you playing, Snug?" asks Thinky, lying next to her.

Sparky flops down beside them. "Phew! I need a rest! Can I join in too?"

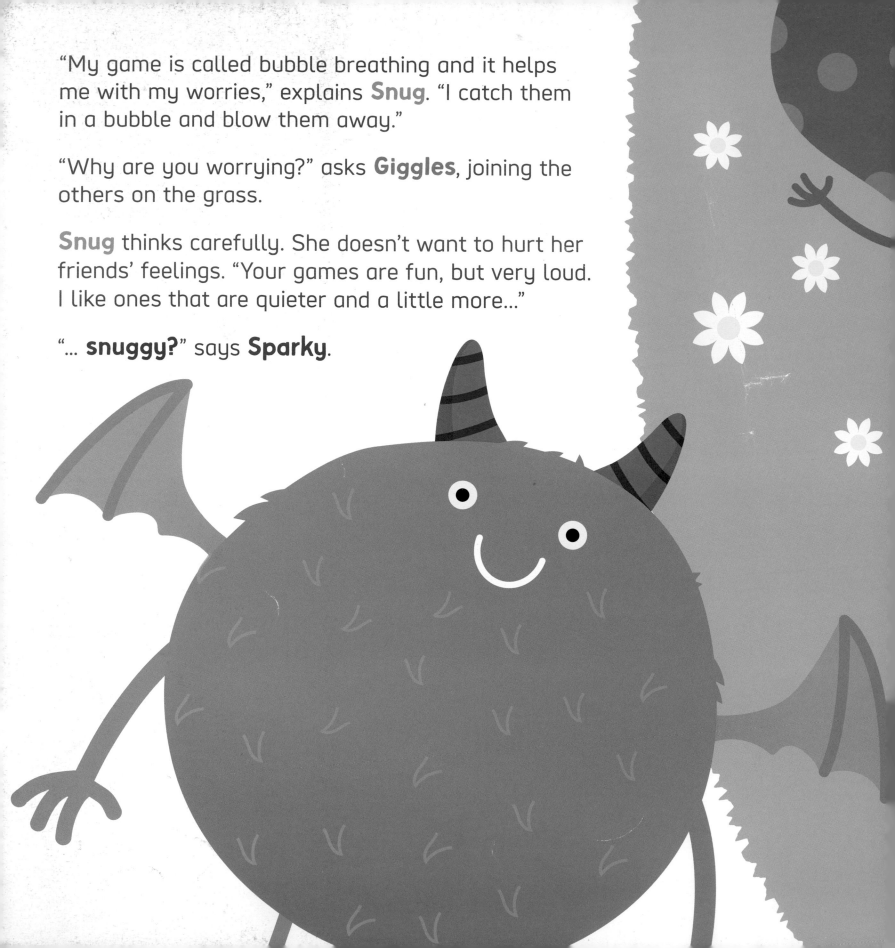

"My game is called bubble breathing and it helps me with my worries," explains **Snug**. "I catch them in a bubble and blow them away."

"Why are you worrying?" asks **Giggles**, joining the others on the grass.

Snug thinks carefully. She doesn't want to hurt her friends' feelings. "Your games are fun, but very loud. I like ones that are quieter and a little more..."

"... **snuggy?**" says **Sparky**.

The monsters look up at the sky and try to think of a quiet, **snuggy** game that they can all play together.

The friends lie very still, then **Snug** points up. "Hey, **Giggles**," she says. "That cloud looks just like you!"

"Oh, yes! I can see all my little legs," replies **Giggles**.

"I can see you too, **Snug** – there!" says **Sparky**. "Look, it's got your wings! And that one next to you looks like me, with all my wavy tentacles."

But **Thinky** is very quiet. There are no clouds anywhere in the sky that look like him. "I can't see my cloud monster," he says, sadly.

Snug notices that **Thinky**'s horns are drooping. Does he feel left out too?

She spots two fluffy round clouds rolling across the sky. "Those clouds look like your amazing wheels, **Thinky**!"

A toothy grin spreads across **Thinky**'s face. "I love **whizzing** around on my wheels!"

Thinky's horns are pointy again – he's had a fun idea. He shows his friends how fast he can roll, making circles in the grass.

Wheeeee!

"That game was fun." **Sparky** sighs. "I feel all ... floaty!"

Snug flies a loop in the sky. "Me too!" she says with a smile.

"Being **snuggy** is just right after being all..." **Thinky** tries to find the right word.

Giggles pulls his best funny face. "**Monstery**!" he adds.

After a fun day together, it's time for the monsters to go home.

"**Thinky**!"

"**Sparky**!"

"**Giggles**!"

"And **Snug**!"

"Let's say goodbye with a **monster hug**!"

Tucked up in bed, **Snug** gets even more **snuggy**.

She takes a big breath in – one, two, three – and then out, with a quiet bedtime **ROAR**!

Bye-bye, bedtime worries!
She imagines them
floating out of the window
and into the night...

Zzzz-shew!
Zzzz-shew!
Zzzz-shew!

Snug's roars soon become **snore-roars**
as she drifts off to sleep – all ready for
the next adventure with her friends.

mindful monsters

Be in the moment together!

Create magic mindfulness moments anytime, anywhere.

Help your child develop life skills

Doing regular mindfulness exercises is proven to help children understand their emotions, build resilience, achieve a sense of calm and improve focus. If your child has a favourite mindfulness activity, encourage them to try it as many times as they like!

Let them come to you

Rather than suggesting to your child that you try a new activity, why not begin doing it yourself. Your little one is likely to ask what you are up to and join in.

Talk about feelings and emotions

Check in with your child after each activity to see how it made them feel. Keep the conversation open and relaxed so your child feels comfortable sharing their thoughts.

All about mindfulness

☺ **Concentration exercises,** like balancing on one leg or going for a barefoot walk, help children to develop an awareness of their bodies and surroundings.

☺ **Creativity exercises,** like dancing or painting pictures, help children to express themselves and their emotions.

☺ **Positivity exercises,** like giving compliments and sharing smiles, promote positive thinking, kindness and gratitude.

☺ **Relaxation exercises,** like cloud spotting and bubble breathing, bring children a moment of calm and can stop racing thoughts.

Ready to try Mindful Monsters?

Mindful Monsters is a fun and exciting way to introduce your children to mindfulness.

Focusing on four key areas the Mindful Monsters subscription aims to boost creativity, improve concentration, inspire positivity and aid relaxation.

It gives you that extra special quality time together while offering brilliant benefits for the whole family. Visit **www.mindfulmonsters.co.uk** to find out more.